KT-407-164

*To the wonderful humans at McIntyre's, and indie booksellers
everywhere, who always choose perfect books
C.S.*

*To Dad, Cathy, and Thiago for brightening
my life with books
M.M.*

First published in the UK 2022 by Walker Books Ltd
87 Vauxhall Walk, London SE11 5HJ

2 4 6 8 10 9 7 5 3 1

Text © 2022 Carlie Sorosiak
Illustrations © 2022 Manu Montoya

The right of Carlie Sorosiak and Manu Montoya to be identified as author and
illustrator respectively of this work has been asserted in accordance with the
Copyright, Designs and Patents Act 1988

This book has been typeset in Bell MT.

Printed in China

British Library Cataloguing in Publication Data: a catalogue record for this
book is available from the British Library

ISBN 978-1-5295-1071-3

www.walker.co.uk

BOOKS AREN'T FOR EATING

Carlie Sorosiak

illustrated by Manu Montoya

WALKER BOOKS

AND SUBSIDIARIES

LONDON • BOSTON • SYDNEY • AUCKLAND

Leopold collected two things that he loved very, very much:
warm jumpers (with goats on them, of course) and …

BOOKS!
(Once he learned not to eat them.
And how to turn the pages.)

Sometimes he imagined himself *inside* the books he read.

He was a pirate!

A figure skater!

An astronaut, gently
floating through space.

It was comforting to become these characters,
to live in their worlds.

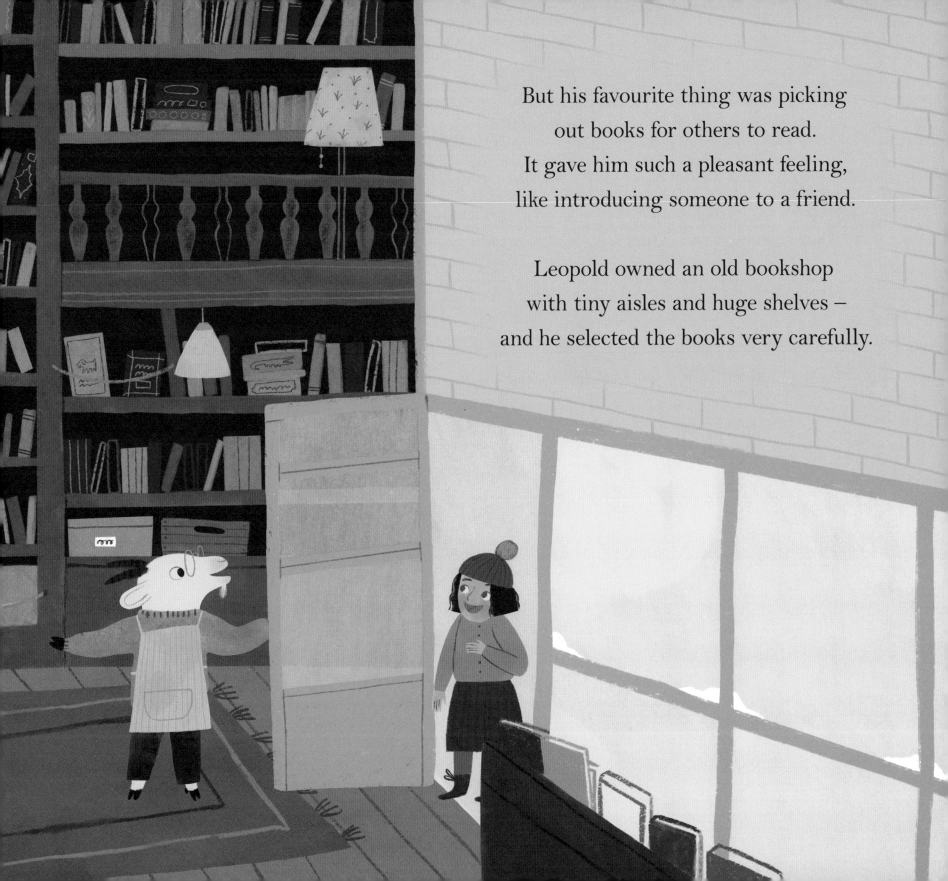

But his favourite thing was picking
out books for others to read.
It gave him such a pleasant feeling,
like introducing someone to a friend.

Leopold owned an old bookshop
with tiny aisles and huge shelves –
and he selected the books very carefully.

For the witty woman in
the feathered hat, he suggested
a book about birds.
Crows, Leopold thought,
are clever, too.

A man in a grey coat
said he'd like to laugh
with his whole belly,
so Leopold found a novel
about gnomes – which
was very funny indeed.

He chose an adventure tale
for the girl in wellies.
She had the spirit of
an explorer.

He recommended books about everything:

hula hoops,

faraway places,

dogs of the
world.

Each fit its reader snugly and warmly like a jumper.

This made Leopold happy.

Most of his customers were human.
But one day, Leopold was overjoyed to see ...

another goat walking
into the shop!

"How may I help you?" Leopold asked.
"I'd like a nice book, if you'd be so kind," said the goat.
"I have just the thing!" said Leopold.

In the back room, Leopold selected a story from his special collection.

"Very good," said the goat.

Then he ate the pages.

"No!" Leopold cried. "Books aren't for eating!"

"Oh dear," said the goat. "I'm terribly sorry. What are they for then?"

So Leopold resolved to show him.
He would find the *perfect* book –
for reading.

Not for eating.

He searched far and wide, through stack after stack.

He even used the tall ladder.

"How's this?"
"Excellent!"
CHOMP, CHOMP!

"What about this?"
"Brilliant!"
MUNCH, MUNCH!

Book after book after book …
the goat ate them all.

"This is going on your bill," said Leopold.
"Goodbye," said the goat.

At dinner that night, Leopold's wife asked him about work.
"I had a tricky customer," Leopold said. "He kept eating the books!"

"Well, so did you once," said his wife.
"That was a long time ago," Leopold said.
But it gave him an idea.

The next morning, when the goat came back, Leopold was ready.

"This was my *favourite* book," he said. "The first one I didn't eat.
It excited me, challenged me, and made me feel less alone."

The goat looked at the book.
And looked.
And opened his mouth…

Suddenly, the book flipped open to page one.
"Oh!" said the goat.

He read the first line,
then the next, and the next…

He couldn't stop.

All day, he curled up in the shop and read.

Leopold smiled, his heart aglow. "I'll pick out some more for you tomorrow."
"Thank you," the goat said. "These stories fill me up."

Some books are just too good to eat.